This Faber book belongs to

....

FABER & FABER

has published children's books since 1929. Some of our very first publications included *Old Possum's Book of Practical Cats* by T. S. Eliot, starring the now world-famous Macavity, and *The Iron Man* by Ted Hughes. Our catalogue at the time said that 'it is by reading such books that children learn the difference between the shoddy and the genuine'. We still believe in the power of reading to transform children's lives.

For lovabubble Lizzie, adorabubble Jess and irreplaceabubble John
C. F.

For Annie & Casper
A. M.

First published in the UK in 2017, first published in the US in 2018 by Faber and Faber Limited, Bloomsbury House, 74–77 Great Russell Street, London WC1B 3DA. Text copyright © Clare Foges, 2017. Illustration copyright © Al Murphy, 2017. ISBN 978-0-571-34045-3 All rights reserved. Printed in China.
1 3 5 7 9 10 8 6 4 2
The moral rights of Clare Foges and Al Murphy have been asserted. A CIP record for this book is available from the British Library.

BATHROOM BOOGIE

WRITTEN BY
CLARE FOGES

ILLUSTRATED BY
AL MURPHY

When you kids go off to school,
And grown-ups go to work...

Your bathroom comes ALIVE
And all the things there go berserk!

The tiles become a dance floor,
The light a disco ball ...

It's called the
BATHROOM BOOGIE
The most splashy bash of all!

SPLOT

TOOTHPASTE is the party king!
He loves to sing and shout.

He wriggles and he squeezes,

Until half his paste comes out!

MOUTHWASH is the coolest dude—
Check out his minty moves!

He backflips on the bath mat...
And he shows them how to groove!

SO shake it in the shower,
Tap dance on the tap!
Wiggle like a washcloth,
HEY!
And do the shampoo rap!

With twisty neck and silver suit...
Here comes the
POWER SHOWER!
He swings that neck from left to right—
It's shower's happy hour!

Every time he swings his head,
And FLICKS and FLOPS and FLIPS...
The shower gels run underneath
And rain dance in the drips!

The bubble bath is naughty!
She laughs when she's in trouble...

And every time she giggles—
POP! Out comes another bubble!

The **TOOTHBRUSHES** are ravers,
They blow on little whistles!
The sink becomes a mosh pit,
Where they headbang with their bristles...

PEEEP

SO shake it in the shower,
Tap dance on the tap!
Wiggle like a washcloth,
HEY!
And do the shampoo rap!

The **BATH**
becomes a pool party!
The **SPONGES** dive right in!

They team up with the
COTTON BUDS,
And synchronize a swim!

The LOOFAHS go bananas —
They dance like they don't care!
They limbo on the toilet lid...
And backflip through the air!

The **SPONGES** and the **WASH CLOTHS** Are the very best of friends...

They do the hokey-pokey 'Til the bathroom boogie ends!

So if you're in the bathroom
And you notice something's moved...

You'll know it's from this party,
When your bathroom loves to groove!